Blossom
Saves the Day

Book 3 in the Blossom and Matilda Series

By Starla Criser

Illustrated by Sharon Revell

Special thanks to Angie.
-S.C.

For information regarding permission, write to Starla Enterprises, Inc.,

Attention: Permissions Department,
9415 E. Harry St., Ste. 603, Wichita, KS 67207

ISBN: 978-1719528115

Printed in the U.S.A

Blossom loves summer and being outside.

But the other cows were heading back to the barn. Even her friends had returned to the farmyard.

"Come on, Blossom," Elsie called out.

She dragged her feet.

1

Something made her stop walking.

The sky was turning dark.

The clouds were spinning.

She smelled rain.

Lightning sparked a jagged line.

"Oh no! Oh no! Oh no!"

Elsie and the other cows had also stopped.

They looked around in confusion.

Blossom knew their farm was in danger!

The family... her animal friends.

"Run!" she yelled.
"Back to the field!"

4

They raced away.
Not Blossom.

She had to find her farm family.

Blossom saw Katie and Annie jumping rope in the farmyard.

They laughed ... not sensing danger.

6

Blossom sped toward them.
Her heart raced.

"Moo, moo, moo!"
she called out.

She meant,

"Stop! Go! Danger!"

They saw the spinning clouds.

"Go the the shelter! NOW!"
Farmer Sam yelled to his daughters.

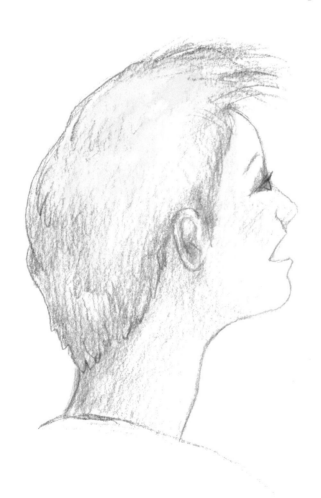

Blossom was happy that they'd seen the danger coming.

"Go to the field, Blossom!" he yelled.
"Be safe there!"

But she couldn't leave until she found her friends.

Steve was with Matilda and Priscilla
by the henhouse.

They didn't see the storm
coming their way.

Blossom ran toward them ...
scared for her friends.

"Run! To the far
end of the field!

"Go now! RIGHT NOW!"

They looked at her in confusion.
They didn't move.

"What? Why?"
Steve yelled.

"A bad storm is coming!"
Blossom yelled back.

The chickens in the pen started wandering around.

They SQUAWKED, worried.

Blossom hurried to the gate.

She used her nose to lift the latch.

Matilda used her paw to pull the gate open.

When free to go, the chickens raced away.

Blossom looked at her friends.

The smell of rain was stronger.

The clouds were darker.

"Run as fast as you can! Go to Ferdie and Hamish!"

16

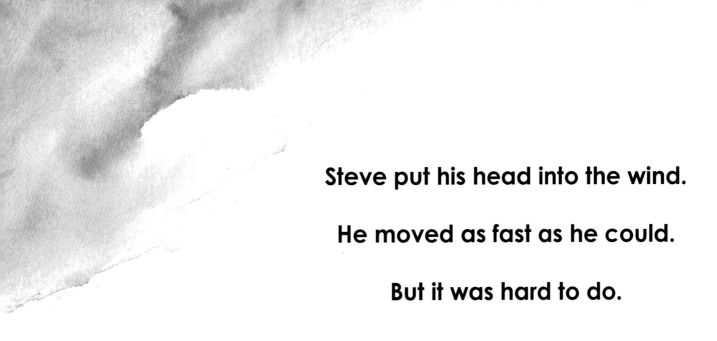

Steve put his head into the wind.

He moved as fast as he could.

But it was hard to do.

Matilda started to follow Steve, but she stopped to look back.

Priscilla hadn't moved.

Priscilla sat with her wings wrapped around her.

She shivered. Her eyes huge in worry.

18

"We have to go!" Blossom shouted. "It isn't safe here."

"I ... I can't!" Priscilla said, sounding scared.

19

Matilda took charge of their friend.

She nudged Priscilla's bottom.

"MOVE!"

Blossom was glad when they made it to the corner of the field.

Ferdie called out, "I'm happy to see you all!"

He saw Matilda looking frightened.

"Come here, my furry friend," Ferdie yelled

21

Matilda ran to him and crawled
under Ferdie's big body.

He would do his best
to protect her.

22

Hamish saw Priscilla
shivering in fear.

"Come here, lass!"

He knocked down a
fence post to get to her.

23

Steve couldn't get to anyone for protection. He fought to stand in the strong wind.

The sky was almost black.
Thunder rumbled.
Lightnig flashed.

Blossom hoped they would
be okay.

**Should they have
gone to the barn?**

The wind knocked
Steve off his feet.

He tumbled until his
leg hit a fence post.
"SQUAWK!"

The wind blew Matilda out from under Ferdie.

"Meow!" she cried.

He caught her with his teeth
and pulled her back to him.

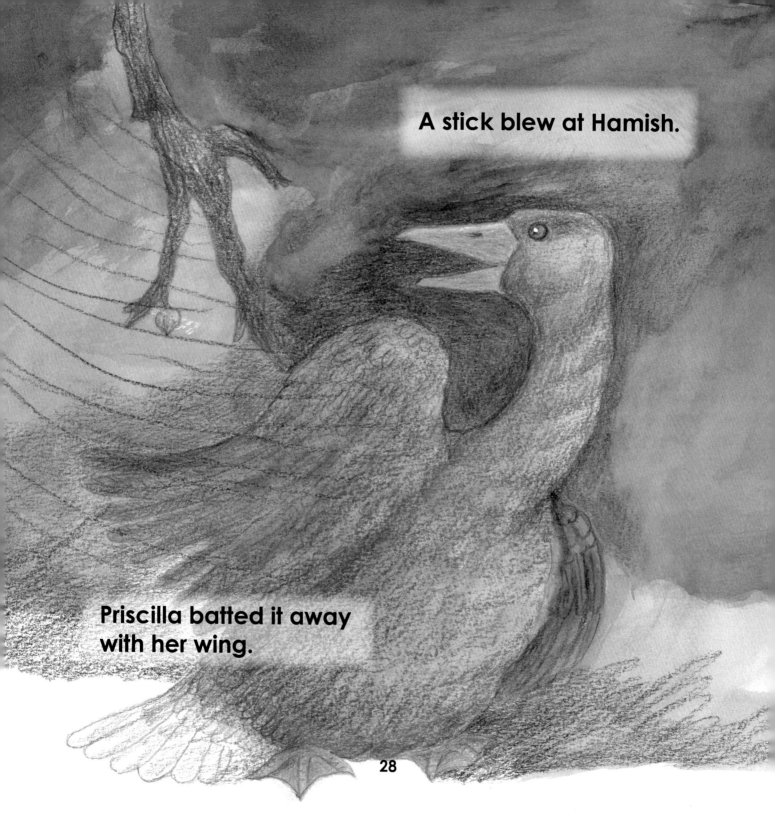

A stick blew at Hamish.

Priscilla batted it away
with her wing.

28

Finally the storm ended. They watched the sky clear.

A rainbow came out.

Blossom was happy none of them had been hurt too bad.

29

Ferdie knew Blossom was worried about the farm family.

"Go check on your other family."

She wanted to go to them.

But she had to be sure her friends were okay.

She looked down at Steve
as he hopped on one leg.

"I'll get you help,
my friend."

"We'll ALL get him help," Priscilla said.

"Climb onto my back."

Matilda shoved Steve
onto Priscilla's back.

"Thanks,"
Steve said, struggling.

Blossom led her friends back to the farmyard.

She was happy they had survived the storm.

But she worried about the farm family.

The barn had been hit by the storm.

The roof stood
high into the air.

Other parts were
broken too.

It was good that they hadn't
been inside the barn.

The family's truck had been wrapped around a tree.

Chickens stood in the farmyard ... not sure what to do.

Their hen house was gone.

"Where is the family?" Blossom asked in fear.

"Please be okay." She hurried toward the still closed storm shelter.

"Please be okay."

The door opened and Farmer Sam climbed out.

He helped out his wife, Katie and Annie.

Blossom didn't care about the damage they'd seen.

Her farm family was okay!

"There's Blossom!" Katie yelled.

"And Matilda!" Annie cried out.

"Oh dear," the girl's mother said. She looked at Priscilla carrying Steve.

"Our poor rooster got hurt."

"We'll take care of him."
Farmer Sam smiled as his wife
held Steve.

"It could have
been so much
worse."

"Our sweet Blossom saved us
all with her wild mooing."

40

Blossom MOOED again ...
happily this time.

She would always do
anything to protect her
friends and family.

Stay tuned for more adventures
with Blossom and her friends!

Made in the USA
Lexington, KY
18 September 2018